¿Qué hora es? / Let's Tell Time

# Es hora de ir a la escuela

# It's Time for School

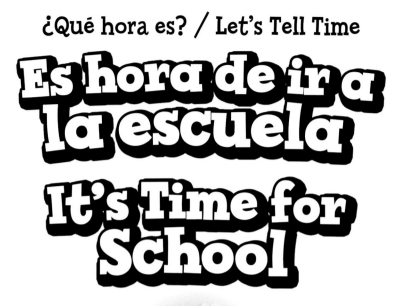

Rosaura Esquivel

traducido por / translated by Alberto Jiménez

ilustrado por / illustrated by
Brian Garvey

New York

Published in 2018 by The Rosen Publishing Group, Inc.
29 East 21st Street, New York, NY 10010

First Edition

Translator: Alberto Jiménez
Editorial Director, Spanish: Nathalie Beullens-Maoui
Editor, English: Theresa Morlock
Book Design: Raúl Rodriguez
Illustrator: Brian Garvey

Cataloging-in-Publication Data

Names: Esquivel, Rosaura.
Title: It's time for school = Es hora de ir a la escuela / Rosaura Esquivel.
Description: New York : PowerKids Press, 2018. | Series: Let's tell time = ¿Qué hora es? | In English and Spanish | Includes index.
Identifiers: ISBN 9781508157038 (library bound)
Subjects: LCSH: Schools–Juvenile fiction.
Classification: LCC PZ7.E888 It 2018 | DDC [E]–dc23

Manufactured in the United States of America

CPSIA Compliance Information: Batch #BS17PK: For further information contact Rosen Publishing, New York, New York at 1-800-237-9932

# Contenido

# Contents

El despertador de Myka suena a las 7:00.
¡Es hora de prepararse para ir a la escuela!

Myka's alarm clock goes off at seven o'clock.
It's time to get ready for school!

El autobús escolar recoge a Myka a las 8:00. Myka debe llegar a la parada a tiempo, ¡si no lo perderá! Su papá espera con ella a que venga el autobús.

At eight o'clock the school bus picks Myka up. She has to make sure to be at the bus stop on time, or else she will miss it! Myka's dad waits with her until the bus shows up.

Myka llega a la escuela a las 9:00.

At nine o'clock Myka arrives at school.

Al ver a su amigo Tony, se acerca corriendo a saludarlo. Tony y Myka están en la misma clase.

She spots her friend Tony and runs over to say hello. Tony and Myka are in the same class.

La profesora de Myka se llama señorita Kelleher.
Lee los nombres de los alumnos de una lista,
a fin de comprobar que todos están en clase
preparados para aprender.

Myka's teacher's name is Ms. Kelleher. She reads each student's name from a list to make sure that everybody is in class and ready to learn.

A las 10:00 la clase habla sobre el clima.

At ten o'clock, the class talks about the weather.

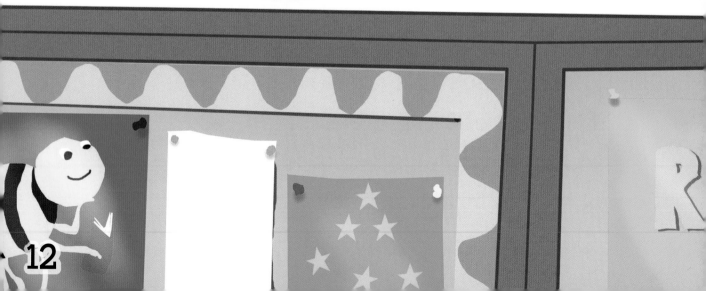

12

El día está gris y nuboso. ¡Puede que llueva!

Today it is gray and cloudy outside. It looks like rain!

A las 11:00 es hora de la clase de música. La clase de música es la preferida de Myka.

At eleven o'clock it's time for music class. Music class is Myka's favorite part of the day.

Ella toca el piano mientras Tony canta.

She plays the piano while Tony sings a song.

Después de clase de música
llega la hora de los trabajos
de ciencia.

After music class it's time
to work on science projects.

Myka y Tony están haciendo una maqueta.

Myka and Tony are making a diorama.

A las 12:00 la clase va a la
cafetería para almorzar.

At twelve o'clock the class
goes to the cafeteria
for lunch.

El papá de Myka le ha puesto una sorpresa en la lonchera: ¡un delicioso albaricoque!

Myka's dad packed a surprise in her lunchbox, a tasty apricot!

Después de comer, Myka y sus amigos escuchan a la señorita Kelleher leer un cuento sobre un tigre.

After lunch Myka and her friends listen to Ms. Kelleher read a story about a tiger.

A Myka le gustan las ilustraciones llenas de color.

Myka likes the colorful pictures in the book.

A las 2:00 de la tarde termina el día en la escuela.

At two o'clock the school day is over.

¡Es hora de volver a casa! A Myka
le encanta ser alumna de kinder.

It's time to go home! Myka loves
being a kindergartener.

# Palabras que debes aprender
# Words to Know

(el) despertador
alarm clock

(la) maqueta
diorama

(la) lonchera
lunchbox

# Índice / Index

24